KENJI

KENJI

THE BOY FROM THE UNDERWORLD

Randy Vidal

Charleston, SC
www.PalmettoPublishing.com

Kenji

First Edition

Paperback ISBN: 979-8-8229-2193-1
eBook ISBN: 979-8-8229-2194-8

CHAPTER 1

Living and dying are both parts of being human, right? People are born and try to live their lives to the fullest. "Live your life to the fullest…You only live once." That is what I hear everyone saying. But this is not the case for me. In this world, people are born with gifts. One can have super strength or speed or be really intelligent. Some people are born with more than one gift. There are also those who are handed power from someone else. And last but not least, there are those who are born without gifts. To me, those people are the unluckiest ones. They are in a world where your gift, your power, is everything, and they are powerless. They are looked down upon. They call them the powerless. The powerless people are placed far under the city because the big city is no place for them; they just don't fit in. So how can you live your life to the fullest when you're living in the underworld?

You can't!

I was born into a family with no gifts. For someone who was born in such a dangerous world, I never had so much as a scratch on my body. A lot of people called me lazy and said that I never did anything to help the people of the underworld. But they don't really know. I was the hardest worker in this ugly world. They said that I didn't do anything, but in reality, they were the ones who didn't do anything. They sat on their asses every day, complaining about how life, the world, God, and everything else was unfair to them. But that was not me. If someone was better

1

than I was, it meant that they worked harder. Still, I will not deny that some people are born talented.

I believe that those above are the ones who were born talented. They never had to work for anything. From the moment they were given their gifts, they walked around with a silver spoon in their mouths. I hated them. I hated them because they acted all high and mighty, yet they didn't know how hard the world was down here for someone like me or for people like us, the people of the underworld.

It was a day like any other. I helped my dad build a new home for us. I didn't have much else to do since we had no school down here or much of anything else. So I was happy to help him. He always told me to be careful since I could really hurt myself with the tools that we used to build. It was especially hard to build in the underworld because we didn't get much sun down here or much light in general. I was nailing up the wood for the house. I didn't pay attention to what I was doing, and I accidentally hammered a nail through my hand. I screamed. The pain was unbelievable. Then I realized there was no pain. It was all in my head. I looked at my hand. And the nail was still in it, yet I felt no pain. I took the nail out and still no pain. When I looked at my hand, it was healing. I was shocked. "I'm gifted," I hissed. I was disgusted with myself. I could not believe I was one of those people I hated.

I could not believe I was gifted. I am someone who was born with nothing and was struggling to live day to day. I guess being in shock blocked me from seeing it. But when I looked down, there was a drop of my blood on the ground. I tried to wipe it with my hand, and it burned. At first, it hurt a lot, but then it didn't. I looked at my hand, and it looked like it was burned. Then, just like before, it was like nothing had happened. I cleaned the other drop off and left. I needed to tell someone, but who? Down here, everyone was looked down upon by the ones above. I decided I should just keep it to myself. It was not like there was anyone who would care about me enough to stick their neck out for me. No one really cared about anyone in the underworld. I thought, Maybe I'll just leave. It is not like anyone will miss me.

I walked home, and I thought about who I should talk to. I wondered if there was anyone I could talk to. The world was full of selfishness. As long as there is a concept of good and winners, there will always be the vanquished. And those who are vanquished have nothing left to live for. No one here would accept me. I made up my mind to leave this place. It was not like the people here would want me to stay. We were banished for a reason.

When I got home, I saw my mother sitting outside in her wheelchair. When I was little, I always used to talk to my mother. I told her jokes, and I laughed. But she never did. Now that I look back at it, I remember my mother never said a word to me. Father was always taking care of her. It was like she couldn't move or do things on her own. It was as if she were dead, yet she was not yet gone. I didn't really know if my mother was alive. Sometimes I would wonder what she was thinking. I wondered if she even knew that I was her son. Sometimes I would play with her tight, curly hair. At times, her smile became as bright as the little rays of light that sneaked in from the surface. At times, I wondered what the surface was like. Maybe my mother wanted to see it just as much as I did.

The next morning, I gathered all the things I thought I needed and left home. I took all the money I had, which was only $702.22. I also packed my nicest clothes. I believed that if I wore them, maybe I might not stand out; maybe I'd fit right in.

"Why are you packing your things, boy?" asked Father as soon as he got home.

"I'm going to the world above," I quickly replied.

"The apple doesn't fall far from the tree," said my father. "You know…before you were born, your mother had the same dream. But unlike all of us from the underworld, she did have a little gift. She was able to heal all the little wounds that you had," Father continued.

"Is that why I don't have any scars?" I asked.

"Yeah," he responded, "when you were just a little kid, she used to love playing with your curly hair. One day you went outside to play, and your mother got worried that you were not home. I also wondered where you were. We went looking for you late at night. Yet you were nowhere to be found," Father said in a very sad voice.

"Where was I?" I curiously continued to ask questions.

"You had fallen off a small cliff. As you know, the underworld is not a beautiful place. You had gone to play, and you must have fallen. When we found you, you were nearly unrecognizable. There was a pool of blood beneath you. It was like your body had almost exploded from the impact. Yet somehow, your heart still had a beat. Your mother tried her hardest to heal you, but her power did not seem to be strong enough to heal you completely. For days, she tried and tried again. I just watched helplessly." My father punched the wall. His fist started bleeding. "She put everything she had into saving you, and she did. But at a cost. Her power was not to bring people back from near-death. It was just healing a small cut or minor disease. Yet she saved you; she gave her life away to bring you back from that state. Since that day, she hasn't spoken or walked," said Father.

I couldn't help but feel saddened by this. Tears fell from my eyes. I don't remember this ever happening to me. I felt deep pain in my heart, yet my gift would not cure me. I looked at my father's face. He seemed so sad.

"I am so sorry, Son. I am your father. Still I couldn't save you and your mother. Even though she lives, her life is not what it once was. Please do not blame yourself. For you did nothing wrong," he added.

I held his bleeding hand and said sadly, "You have nothing to be sorry about. I know you must have felt terrible while this was happening."

"I must go now," I said to my father.

"When you get to the gates, let the gatekeeper know who you are, and he will let you pass. When you reach the world above, look for a place called Power Academi. There you might learn things about yourself and your new power," said Father, looking at the hand that I had healed.

He had this look on his face, as if this wasn't news to him.

As I walked to the gate, I wondered how my life would change. I would be enrolling in a new school, in a new place, and living a new life. I knew that all of this could be exciting, but I had to keep my goal in mind. I had to learn how to use my powers to bring back my mother from her dead state. Before I left, Father told me that my mother's condition was getting worse by the day. She was using what she had left of her power to keep herself from dying. Still at the rate that she was going, she would be dead in a year. I had to learn how to use my power before then.

When I made it to the gate, I saw that there was a long line of people. I wondered what they were there for. When I got closer to the line, I realized that they were all men, men of all ages.

"Why are you all here?" I asked one of the boys in line.

"This is the line to leave the underworld. We are all here to walk across the gates to the world above," the boy replied.

"I thought you had to be gifted to go into the world above," I said to the boy.

"You do. Most of us are just here because we want out of this miserable place. There is no food, no education; it is full of violence, and there's no form of justice. Everyone here only cares about themselves and what is theirs," the boy answered in what seemed to be anger.

"Everyone here is gifted?" I asked curiously.

"No. None of us are gifted. As you know, you are either born with one or given one by some who had one. We are not that lucky. We are just here to fake having power and see if we can pass," said the boy. "We just want to be free of this world," he continued.

I replied with silence. I looked the boy in the eyes, and he looked back. His eyes filled with tears.

"I'm sure you are here for the same reason. Good luck!" said the boy with a forced smile on his face.

I made my way to the back of the line and waited. The line moved forward very fast. I saw a lot of guys turning back with what seemed a face full of terror. I was only about five spaces back from the boy I talked to. When I saw his face, he looked scared; it was like he knew death was coming for him. As we got closer to the gate, I began to hear screams. The closer I got, the louder they became. Once I was close enough, I saw what was truly happening. These men were being killed and then brought back to life. Now it was the boy's turn.

"What is your gift now, boy?" asked one of the gatekeepers.

"Super strength," said the boy.

"Why do you keep coming back, boy? I hate doing this to you," asked the gatekeeper.

"I need to help my family!" shouted the boy.

"Very well then." The gatekeeper picked up a humongous rock. He then proceeded to throw it at the boy. The boy tried to catch the rock, but it was hopeless. It was way too heavy for him, and he was crushed by it. The scream reached my heart, and I froze. Again that sharp pain reached me, and it was the one that would not heal. The gatekeeper lifted the rock, and all I saw was a pool of blood. His body was unrecognizable. I couldn't tell who he was anymore. The second gatekeeper walked up to the body and with his fingertips touched it.

"Rewind," whispered the second gatekeeper. The splatter of blood and the skin that splashed everywhere began to move back to the main body. It was like the body was moving back in time. Then the boy was back. He was fine, or at least he looked fine physically. Mentally he seemed as if he were dead. When he was walking back, he looked at me, and our eyes met just like the last time. All I saw was fear. The rest of the guys in front of me left the line. I assumed that they were just too scared to die.

"Next!" screamed the first gatekeeper.

I walked up to him still in shock at what had just happened to that boy.

"How old are you, boy?" one of the gatekeepers asked. It was the one who slashed me.

"I'm seventeen," I replied.

"Why is it that you wish to leave the underworld?" he asked.

"My mother is dying. I wish to enroll at the power high school in the world above. There I will learn to use my power. After that, I will come back and help my dying mother," I answered.

"What is your power?" they both asked, speaking at the same time.

"I'm not sure. I just healed all my wounds and healed my father. My blood also fell on the ground and burned it," I answered.

The gatekeepers looked at each other for a second. Then they ran straight at me. I closed my eyes and tried to move out of the way, but I was too slow. When I opened my eyes, there were two swords going right through me. I screamed in excruciating pain. I fell to the floor, and for a brief moment, I was unable to move. I lay on the floor for a second thinking that this was the end for me and Mother. But then I thought of the pain my father had been going through all those years. I grabbed one of the swords that was piercing my chest. I pulled with all my strength and struggled to pull it out. The pain was unbearable. I could see the rest of the people in line who had gotten there after me run away until there was no one left. When the first sword came out, I tried to pull the second one out. The pain was not going away. Still I struggled and pulled. When the second one came out, I screamed in pain. Then the pain was gone. I stood up, and just like my hand and my father's fist, my chest healed. The swords, which were covered in my blood, had melted. The only thing left was the handle, and even that was starting to disintegrate. The gatekeepers came at me again with two other swords. This time though, I didn't do anything, not a single thing. I took them out, and my wounds healed immediately. I'm not sure why the first time hurts so bad, and then it doesn't hurt at all. They kept cutting me and stabbing me, yet I felt no pain. Weapon after weapon, they melted away.

"Wow, so there really is someone here with actual power," said the first keeper.

"I guess there is." I laughed.

"You can call me Ichiro, and this is my twin brother, Jiro," said Ichiro.

"It's nice meeting you," I said.

"So you say that you want to enroll in the Power high school so that you can learn to use your powers and save your mom?" asked Jiro, looking directly at me.

"Yes!" I answered quickly with a serious look on my face. I found myself calm. I had no fear in me, for they could no longer hurt me. My power was beyond theirs. I think they understood this as well. Ichiro and Jiro looked at each other and then looked at me and laughed.

"We like your spirit, boy!" said Ichiro and Jiro nodded and smiled

"I will be the one to take you there," said Jiro. " I am very interested in your power. I also want to see the extent of your power and what you will do once you reach that level. I assume that there is no one waiting for you on the other side. So you will stay with me while you attend school, and when you are ready, I will bring you back," Jiro continued.

"Thank you! I promise you that you shall not regret this!" I was full of excitement. Now, at the very least, I had a place to stay and someone who could answer questions as they came along.

"All right. We leave now," said Jiro.

"Right," I replied.

We walked for a little while before Ichiro stopped us. "What was your name, boy?"

"Oh, my name...I am Kenji. Kenji of the Underworld."

CHAPTER 2

As I walked, the memory of that boy came to me. I felt saddened by it. I could not believe that day in and day out, children and adults, all types of men, were going there just to die and be brought back to life. This made me think about the world I lived in. Was it really that bad? I knew that there was violence, I knew that there was very little food or water, and I also knew that the chance of survival was very low. But to come back every day to keep dying over and over. That had to break them.

"Jiro, how does your power work?"

Jiro sighed. We had been walking for a while, and we were also very hungry.

"You know people don't usually talk about their powers to others. But since I will be going as your father in the world above, then it's right that you should know. My power is time manipulation. I can't go back in time, but I can turn things in time. So if I were to touch something or someone, I could turn back their time to when they were a child or not even alive. I can also touch a body and bring it back to a point when it was alive."

He continued, "Also, Kenji, the people of the world above do not like the people from the world underneath them. They believe that you are less capable and that your power will be very weak. But you will be one of the strongest kids there."

"But I don't even know how to use my powers."

"Kenji, when I touched you with my sword, I tried to turn back your time, but all that happened was I got blood on me and started to burn. Then when I stabbed you the second time, I tried it again. And it still didn't work, but this time, the burn spots on my hand were gone. So not only did I not hurt you, but you hurt me."

"Oh, it hurts, trust me," I cried.

We walked for a little bit longer, and then we reached a long staircase. There was a small door at the end of the stairs. As we walked up this staircase, I thought about my father. The pain that came over me made me tear up. What if I never found a way to cure my mother? What if all the pain he went through was for nothing? There was a lot of weight on me, and I didn't know how to deal with it. My mother's life was in my hands, and if I failed, she would die. These thoughts filled my head over and over again while I was climbing the staircase. The confidence that I had built up to this point just kept getting weaker and weaker the higher I went up the steps. Maybe I was wrong. What was I thinking? I'm just a kid from the underworld. I am not special. I can't save her. My head was full of negativity. I stopped walking and looked up. There was just a small chunk of steps left for me to climb. Yet my legs felt weak, and these steps felt taller and taller the more I stepped. I looked up one more time and stopped walking. I looked over at Jiro, and he looked right back at me. We didn't say a word to each other. He just kept going up as I sank into despair. I stood still for what felt like minutes.

I took a deep breath and looked up one more time. I saw Jiro at the top of the stairs. He was looking down at me. I felt ashamed. After telling my father I was going to help my mother, I stood there hopelessly begging for someone to help me take the last steps. I couldn't go back now, yet I couldn't move forward either.

"What are you waiting for, Kenji? After walking for this long and the big talk about how you'll be the one to save your mother, how you had to prove to your father that what happened to you and your mother wasn't his fault."

He was right. After talking myself up so much, how could my head be filled with all these negative thoughts.

"*Run, Kenji! Run!*" I screamed as I started sprinting up the long steps.

The more I ran, the more negative things would come to my head. But I just kept running. I could not stop just because of some self-doubt. I had people who were counting on me. I couldn't let them down.

When I made it to the top, Jiro looked at me.

"So you made it...You know, most people turn around at the stairs."

"It wasn't even a problem," I responded.

"The name of the stairs is the Stairs of Despair. They were built here by the higher-ups of the world above. Their purpose is to keep the people down here from just running up to the world above. In the past, people who were weak at heart tried to get up these golden stairs before only to turn back and end their own lives. These stairs filled them with doubt and negativity. They couldn't handle what their head was full of."

"I see, but why didn't you tell me this before I took the first step?" I asked Jiro.

"I just had to make sure that you were strong enough emotionally to be in the world above. When we get there, they will bully you and try to do anything they can to get under your skin." As Jiro talked, his facial expression became more serious. "With all that being said, I'm glad you made it, Kenji. Welcome to Valhalla!"

For the first time since I left home, I smiled knowing that by crossing these doors, I would take my first step to saving Mother. We pushed the doors open. On the other side was a dark room. This room felt cooler than any room I'd ever been in before. We walked down the long hallway and came upon another set of doors, yet these doors were smaller.

Jiro opened the door and said, "Kenji, we will be heading into town now. Please do not get lost on the way there. Stay close, and do not get cut anywhere please…It would be a shame if the plants died."

When I walked out of what seemed like a long tunnel, the first thing I saw was the sun. It was so bright and warm—not burning but warm enough to not feel cold at all. This was the first time I had seen the sun directly. I only looked at the sun for about five seconds, and my eyes started to hurt. Everything went from light to dark really fast. I became a bit scared because I could not see anything anymore.

"Why did you stare directly into the sun for so long? You will go blind."

The darkness was scary. I thought that maybe the sun would make it go away, so I looked at it again. It was so bright, but when I looked away, I was completely blind. How could something so beautiful cause so much pain? I couldn't see anything at this point. Everything was just getting dark.

After a little while of walking, my eyes began to heal. After they healed, it was like I could see better. Everything looked so clear. I am still not sure if that was just how the world above looked.

When I looked at this world, I saw it was truly beautiful. As we walked to the gates of the town, Jiro talked up to the men who were standing at the gate. After a few seconds, Jiro called me over, and we walked into the city. There were all types of people there. There were people of different races and of different colors. There were people in vehicles. There were also people who seemed to be floating in the air and moving in whatever direction they wished. People really high above me were flying at a faster speed than even the vehicles. But to me the most impressive thing was that there were people who were standing still and then out of nowhere took off running so fast all I could see was a blur.

"Speedsters," said Jiro. "They are the fastest beings in the world. There are even ones who are so fast that some say they can go back in time."

I was so amazed at this. There were people with such amazing power that mine seemed so lame. I started looking around and saw that there were some people who were in the alley beating on some other kid. I walked toward them and before I knew it I lost sight of Jiro, I was alone.

"Hey, leave that kid alone."

The boy was a bit bloody but still stood strong.

"And who are you, kid? You must not be from here!"

"I'm Kenji, and I'm from the underworld."

"The underworld?" the group of boys screamed.

"You are not welcome here, Kenji. Why don't you go back to the underworld where you belong? You low-life human. Know your place, Kenji the human."

The three boys ran up to me and stopped about an arm's length away from me. They held their hands out with their palms directed at my face.

"Light!" the three boys screamed.

Right after that, a bright light emerged from their hands. The boys laughed. This light was even brighter than the sun. After my eyes healed, I looked at the boy who was getting beaten up in the back. His face was disappointed. He looked down at the floor and did look as proud as he once did when I first approached the three bullies. After seeing this, I walked right up to the kid who was on the right, and with all my might, I swung my right fist to the right side of his face. The boy fell backward onto the floor. The two other boys looked at me.

"Do you know what you have done? We are members of the proud light race. How dare you hit one of us? Are you human?"

One of the boys ran to me once again.

"Light!"

This one was even brighter than the last, yet my eyes were not affected.

"That will not work on me again, boy. Know your place. I don't care who you are or what you did. You guys are inferior to me, and that is reality. Now that my eyes have healed, your little flashlight won't do anything to me."

"What are you even saying? I am a god next to you. You are inferior!"

As the boy spoke, I felt an evil inside me, like something that had always been there but had never come out until then.

"Light, light, light, *light*!" one of the boys screamed.

Yet again, it did not work. After seeing this, two of the boys left running. As they ran, they screamed at me, "You are no human."

The other boy who remained looked furious. "Come to me, light sword!"

Light fell from the sky directly on the boy's hand. Seconds later, the light took the shape of a sword.

"Today, you will meet your end, human."

I could see that the sword he carried was burning his hand as soon as he grabbed it. Still he charged at me. As he ran to me, I felt myself getting full of darkness. I opened my arms, and let my guard fully down.

"Die, Kenji! You filthy excuse for a human!"

The boy stabbed me through the heart with the sword. After it stabbed me, I felt the light spread throughout my body. I felt the light in me try to come out through different sides of my body until it finally did. The light had come out of my body through my back. Yet I stood still with my arms out. The boy looked up at me. I looked down at him. I was filled with rage.

"Now you will die, human!" He screamed

I smiled at him as we made eye contact. Suddenly, the boy backed away.

"Y-you hav-have…you have a tail and wings? I thought you were a human, Kenji. And now you show your true colors, you demon. How dare you challenge me as a member of the light race! You will not leave Valhalla alive. You are an inferior being."

When I looked behind me, I saw my wings. They were covered in such beautiful black feathers.

"How does it feel to know that someone from the underworld is stronger than you?" I felt such dark energy within me. "You, a member of the light race, are inferior to me. You were so proud of who you were that you didn't bother to ask who I was."

Deep down, I didn't know where this power was coming from or where these wings and tail came from. Yet I fell in love with the power and with this feeling of being able to do whatever I pleased.

I looked at the boy. His white skin turned pale. I felt this dark aura surrounding me. The sword that was going through my chest slowly dissolved back into light and later into nothingness. The pale boy trembled at my feet.

"You are a demon. You are the demon!"

I raised my fist. But before I could even attempt to hit him, he left running. The young boy who was getting bullied was still in the corner. He was now trembling and shaking.

"Are you okay, boy?" I asked him.

He looked up at me, and I smiled at him. I was not sure what to do with him.

"*Thanks!*" yelled the boy as he ran away.

I was a bit confused. Why would he run away from me if I just saved him?

"Kenji? Is that you? I thought I told you to stay close" Jiro looked at me, amazed.

"Yes, it's me."

"What happened to you, kid? Why is there a hole in your shirt?"

I looked down at the hole and saw that the wound the light sword had given me had disappeared. I looked at Jiro. He smiled back at me.

"I knew it was you. I finally found you."

"What are you talking about, Jiro?"

"A few years ago, the god of this world sensed some type of dark energy coming from the underworld. For that reason, he sent us to retrieve that dark energy. But we lost it. Somehow, it just disappeared. We were in the underworld for a while waiting for it to emerge. But who knew it was you? You are such a kind boy who just wants to save his mom. But you are a demon. The last of your kind."

I was in pure shock.

"I'm just a regular human. I'm from the underworld, Jiro. No one has powers down there."

"Although that is true, Kenji…that is also where the strongest demon used to live years ago. They said he had a daughter, so I was expecting a woman, but again, demons live for a long time, so that woman might just be your mother. After all, she was the one who saved you, right?"

"So let me guess: demons are not allowed in Valhalla?"

"Oh no, they are. People just fear them because of their destructive power. But since you don't want to kill anyone, you should be fine."

I sighed. I really didn't want any trouble here, but that was just my luck.

"All right, Kenji, it's time to head home. You will start school tomorrow morning," Jiro said with enthusiasm.

I flapped my wings, and some of my feathers flew out.

"That's a beautiful black, isn't it, Kenji?"

"Indeed it is." I smiled.

I relaxed for a moment, and my wings shrank back into my body. I looked at my tail. It felt like it was just another leg. Although it was skinnier and a bit shorter than my legs, I could control it just like any other body part.

"Are you going to leave your tail out, Kenji?"

"Yeah, I kind of like it."

The reality was that I had tried to pull it back into my body, but it was no use. I wrapped my tail around my waist and walked alongside Jiro.

CHAPTER 3

While walking next to Jiro, I made sure not to lose sight of him. The city was really big, and I would get lost. As I walked though, I couldn't help but to look around. On my way, I saw a girl—or at least that's what I thought she was. She grew wings out of nowhere just as I did. This time, people didn't run away; they actually looked at her and smiled. Her wings were a dark red. They were made of scales and not feathers like mine. Next to hers, my wings looked fragile.

"She's a beast woman," Jiro said as he caught me staring at the girl.

"Beast woman?" I asked.

"Yes, kid. As you might have found out earlier, there are all different types of races in Valhalla. And the beast race is one of them. They have the power to manifest limbs of a creature or beast. That girl that you were just staring at…her beast is a dragon. That's why there are scales on her body and why her wings look very different from yours, demon boy."

"Ohh, I see."

As I see her start to fly away, I notice how beautiful she is. She looks like an angel flying across the sky.

"We are here, Kenji. This is the place where you will be staying with me." Jiro stopped in front of a pretty big gate.

I walked into the house. It looked like it never ended. I had never seen a house so big before. The yard on our side of the house was bigger than the house I had back home.

"You will be staying here, Kenji. This will be your room."

"*This is my room?*" I was speechless.

This room was twice as big as my room back home. And I thought that my room was big back then.

"Jiro...are you rich?" I looked at him intently.

"Ahahaha...I guess you could say something like that. I worked hard for what I have. But that's not what we're here for. You should wash up and come downstairs when you're ready." Jiro walked off.

I walked into the bathroom. Even this bathroom was better than the bathroom in the underworld. I got undressed and walked in, ready to clean myself. I looked around, but I couldn't find anything that turned on the water. I searched for a bit and saw this small lever that had blue on the left and red on the right.

"This must be it," I said in relief.

I cleaned myself up and headed downstairs. When I got there, Jiro seemed to be talking into some device. I stood there and waited for him to be done. I was standing there for a couple of minutes. Two older women came out of the kitchen, and each had a plate on her head.

"Food is ready," one said.

"Thank you," I said as I sat down at the table.

Jiro stopped talking to his device or whatever that thing was. He sat next to me.

"I just finished talking to the headmaster of the school you will be attending. He said you can start tomorrow morning. So please be prepared and behave yourself. He knows that you are a demon, and he will let you study there for now. Now eat, boy."

Jiro and I started to eat. We were in this big house by ourselves eating food that others had prepared for us. It felt very
luxurious. This got me thinking about the trouble my father was
going through back down at home.

As I finished eating, I picked up a cup of water. This water looked so clean. I could see right through. It looked pure,
good—the opposite of the black aura that had emerged from
me earlier that day. I picked up the cup and drank the water. It
was delicious and very refreshing.

"I should go and rest for tomorrow."

"Yes, indeed you should, Kenji boy. But one more thing before you leave. You should be careful of who you show your powers to. Some people might not have a problem with it, but others
might hate you. They will hate you because of your strength and
because of who you are," Jiro said with a solemn expression.

"Yeah, I noticed that the kids ran from me as soon as they saw
who I was."

"Yeah, just be careful. Your uniform will be in your room in
the morning."

"Right...night then, Jiro, and thank you for the food."

"Good night, Kenji."

I headed up the stairs to my room—I said "my room," but I
was not sure if it was even mine. I was just staying there. I wondered why Jiro was doing this for me. I was just a boy who didn't
even know where his powers came from. I lay down on the bed
face down with my head on the pillow, thinking. What is it that
he even gains from this? What if I am not the person he thinks I
am? What if I am not some demon? I never saw my mother have
wigs or a tail or fly. What if I'm nothing special after all?

My head was filled with these questions. Then out of nowhere my wings came to my mind.

"I wonder if I can make them come out at will."

I thought about how my wings felt. I thought about how they felt like just an extra arm or leg. I felt them growing slowly. Suddenly my back burst open, and my wings came out. They were even bigger than before. As I looked in the mirror, I noticed that they had grown from within me and had not just appeared there. I also noticed that there was blood dripping from where they had come out. Seconds later, I healed. I flapped my wings a bit, and some of the black feathers fell out. I picked up one of them. It was such a dark black. I placed it in the light, and the tone did not change. It was still just as black with a beautiful glare. I relaxed, and my wings slid right back into me, opening the hole in my back, which then healed once again. The pain from the hole was pretty bad, but the more I did it, the less pain I felt. At least the second time, it was just a hole with no blood. Still, I felt the muscles in my back were burning and tearing every time I took my wings out. I went back to bed, and before I knew it, I passed out.

"Wake up…" I heard a soft voice.

"Kenji, wake up," I hear again.

"Wake up!"

I opened my eyes, and it was one of the women who brought out the food the previous night.

"Sorry to wake you sir, Kenji, but it's time for you to head on to school now. Your uniform is ready as well," she said.

"Oh okay, thank you!" I replied.

She left. I got up as soon as my body would let me, threw some water on myself, and changed. I wrapped my tail around my waist and headed down stairs.

"Here, Kenji, take this, and eat it on the way," said Jiro.

He handed me two pieces of bread with chicken and some other stuff in between. I took a bite of it, and it was so delicious.

"Thank you!" I said as I walked out of the house.

As soon as I stepped out the door, I realized that I had no idea where this school was.

"Kenji, please step right into the vehicle," said an old man with a nice long and white mustache.

"Oh right. Do you know where school is?"

"Yes, sir, that's where I will be taking you today."

"Thank you!" I got into the long car, and we took off.

This car moved so much faster than I could have walking and even a bit faster than some of the people who flew close to the ground. Still those who flew higher were way faster, and the speedsters were still much faster. For a moment, I sat back and just waited to get there. I closed my eyes, and before I knew it, I was there.

"Kenji, we are here, sir."

"Thank you, mustache man!"

I got out of the car. Before I realized it, everyone around me was staring at me. They all looked like they were my age. Why were they looking at me?

"Where is his tie?"

"Why is his uniform not buttoned all the way up?"

"I-is that a tail?"

I heard a group of girls talking as they tried to hide the fact that they were looking at me.

I left the tie in the car since I didn't know how to tie it. I buttoned my shirt up with one and wrapped my tail around myself once again. When I looked at the school, I was shocked.

"This place is freaking huge!" I screamed.

Everyone looked at me again, and I felt a bit embarrassed.

"Hey, you must be Kenji!"

"Yeah, that's me. Who are you?"

"I am the headmaster of this school. You need to come with me, Kenji. Today will be the day when you will be evaluated to see what class you belong in. Please follow me."

"Right." I followed.

The school seemed so big. The longer I walked within its walls, the smaller I felt. We walked for some time, and as we walked, more and more people would stare at me. And the more I looked back at them, the more I realized that they didn't really like me. Suddenly the headmaster stopped. There were big doors in front of us. He opened the door.

"Please walk right in." He looked me deep in the eyes.

This startled me for a moment. After a few seconds, I walked right in. As I walked in, I noticed that a group of people was already there waiting for us when we got there. They all sat at a semicircular table. The headmaster stood right next to me.

"Your name, boy?" the man sitting in the middle asked in a deep voice.

"And who are you?" I asked.

Suddenly I felt a strong wave of energy push me back. When I looked up, the man's eyes were wide, and he looked at me in anger.

"I said, 'What is your name, boy?'" he shouted.

The wave of energy became even more powerful. Yet I was not intimidated by it.

"My name is Kenji!" I shouted back.

"Step forward, boy."

In the middle of the long table, there was a clear glass. It was so clear that you could see right through it, like it was water in its purest form.

"Walk up to the ball, and place your hand on it."

"Like this?" I asked.

"Yes, now let your power flow into it. It does not have to be a lot, just a bit to know what type of power you have."

"Right, and how would you know that?"

"The ball will change colors when your power goes into it."

I took a deep breath and placed my hand on the ball. I imagined my power flowing to my hand and then from my hand to the ball. Black smoke began to flow from my hand to the ball. Suddenly everyone around me gasped.

"So it is true. I haven't seen that black smoke in years. You really are a demon."

Before I could blink, everyone was on top of me.

"How do we know that you're not here to take over the world like your type did before you?"

It was hard for me to look up with all the people pinning me down. When I finally managed, I noticed a woman was pointing a sword at my mouth.

"How do I know you won't try to kill us?" She looked deep into my eyes with anger.

"You know, you guys are a pain in my ass!" I screamed.

Before I had time to think, anger filled me. Before I realized it, I noticed a black aura start to emerge from me.

"*Get off me!*"

My wings flew out from my back. Everyone was sent flying. And I hovered there flapping my wings. Black feathers were now everywhere. Now I stare down that woman. At this point I felt like a different person. It was as if I were someone else.

"Know your place, lady. If I were here to kill, you would have been gone by now!" I spoke softly.

The woman who had been standing full of pride in front of me was now trembling to benefit me.

"Your eyes…" she said.

"What was that, lady?"

"Your eyes, your tail, your aura, your…wings. They are all black."

"Yes and so what?"

She dropped to her knees and looked down at the floor.

"Now can someone here please show me how to save my mother?"

I looked forward, and the man who had asked my name before was the only one still sitting there looking at me. For a second, we looked at each other. Then he stood up and slowly walked toward me. Then a second later, he appeared right in front of me and said, "I think we should be friends," with a smile.

A second later, I felt a slash across my chest. I jumped back as I felt the pain.

I looked at my chest and saw my blood dripping down. I looked up, and my blood was also dripping from his hand.

"Ahh!" the man screamed. "It burns!" He looked up at me in disbelief. "What is this?"

"Oh, I'm sorry. Did you get burned?" I grinded

"Yes, I actually did!" He stared at his hand.

Seconds later, he took his shirt off and used it to get rid of the blood. I looked around. Everyone was shocked. I took my wings out just to be ready for him to attack me again.

"So this is what pain feels like?"

"He was actually hurt? How is that even possible? He's never bled before!" said the woman who now trembled even more than before. "You really are a monster, you demon!" she continued.

"Listen to me, lady. I didn't mean to hurt your little prince. He touched my blood so he bore the consequences." I was furious.

Everyone began to shout at the same time.

"Headmaster!" the man who touched my blood shouted.

"Yes?" the headmaster responded.

"What is this boy's name?"

"Kenji!" the headmaster shouted.

"This boy, Kenji, is unbelievably strong. I believe he should be in the Zero S class, Headmaster!"

"Zero S!" everyone shouted.

"I agree with you there, Number One," the headmaster responded.

"Number One? What does that mean? I wondered.

"Well, I think we have made a decision then. Class Zero!" the headmaster said.

As he said this, everyone looked at me with hate and left the room.

"Come with me, Kenji! I'll show you around the school."

"Right." I put my wings away once again and walked over to the headmaster.

He opened the door, and I followed him, leaving a mess in the room. We walked for some time, and I realized that this building was way bigger than I had thought. I also noticed that I was lost. I had no idea where I was.

"This will be your classroom, Kenji! Every day, you will come here and learn academics."

"Okay, thank you."

"Also, you will learn about your powers here."

"Great! When do I start?"

"You start next Monday. Also Jiro is waiting outside for you."

"All right."

"Last thing, Kenji...you must be careful with the people of class Zero S. They are not a big fan of the idea of you...Now, follow me. I'll see you out."

I followed the headmaster to the exit, and there was Jiro waiting for me. I said bye to the headmaster, got into the vehicle with Jiro, and headed home. On the way home, I started to think about how I would save my mother.

"So what class were you ranked in, Kenji?"

"Class Zero S, or something like that."

"*Zero S*! Who gave you that rank?"

"I'm not sure who he was, but the headmaster called him 'Number One.'"

"I see! Well, there is nothing we can do about it now. Just try not to pick fights with anyone there. That is the class for the gifted among the gifted and the strong among the strong. Oh, and that kid, Number One, is the strongest student at the academy, so try not to anger him."

"Well, he might be angry at me already. He kind of cut me and burned his hand with my blood."

"*Ahahahaha!*"

CHAPTER 4

The sun ray hit my face and woke me. Only a day had passed since I was placed in class Zero S. As I lay on the bed, I couldn't help but feel a little nervous and anxious about how my day was going to go. There were a lot of things that could go wrong, and failure was a big possibility.

"Also this power…" I whispered to myself. "This power also scares me. At this point, I don't even know what I am."

The really scary part was that I still didn't know the limits of my own power. The last time I used it, I was able to fly. When I really thought about it, I realized every time I used this power, people seemed to tremble and fear me. They feared me more than I feared myself. This power was *terrifying*.

"Kenji?" One of the women knocked on my door. "Your breakfast is ready when you are."

"I'll be right out."

I jumped out of the bed and got into the shower. The warm water calmed me down. Yet it was also a reminder of how little I had back home, how little my father had, how little life my mother had left. Suddenly fear rushed down my spine. Tears fell from my eyes like never before. For the first time in my life, I felt truly sad and scared. For the first time, I didn't see a way out. For the first time in my life, I felt like there was zero chance of success.

What was I thinking? Someone like me could never accomplish this goal.

If my life was on the line, could I go fight for my mother like that kid I met in the underworld? I felt hopeless, and with my own nails, I slashed at my arm. Blood dripped down my hand, onto the shower floor, and down the drain. My arm healed almost instantly. I scratched again and again and again.

"*Aaaahhhh!*" I screamed in frustration.

"Kenji?" Jiro rushed into my room. "Are you okay?"

I wiped my eyes so that it looked like it was just the warm water in my eyes.

"Yeah, I'm fine. I-I just got soap in my eyes!"

"Okay...well come eat when you are ready."

That was close. I couldn't let anyone see this side of me—the miserable, sad, and scared side.

I finished my shower and made my way downstairs.

"Top of the morning, Kenji."

"Hi, Jiro."

"You will be going to the store today. I think it is time for you to learn how the world works here."

I sat down at the table, and a woman brought the food for me.

"Thank you!"

"My pleasure, Mr. Kenji."

The food looked amazing and tasted just as good as it looked. The food here never ceases to amaze me. I ate the food really fast and even asked for seconds. After I ate, I walked outside where a man w as waiting for me. The same man who took me to school.

"Would you like to be in the car, or would you like to fly, sir?"

"Let's take the car."

"Right away then. Let's go shopping."

We got into the car and headed toward town. When we got there, I could not believe my eyes. The number of people there was even more than the last time. I took a closer look. There were people who worked there and used their powers for their jobs. We walked around awhile. We bought food and beverages. We played games and wandered around for what seemed like an eternity. Before I realized it, the sun was going down.

"Kenji...Master Jiro ordered our driver back a little while ago. That means we will have to fly back home."

"Okay, that's fine by me, but can you fly?"

"Sure I can!" He laughed. "Let's head home now. It's already getting dark."

He started to levitate from the ground. This was the first time I had ever seen someone flying so close to me. He was so high up in the sky. I sprouted my wings and shot up into the sky. The way the air felt on my wings was amazing.

"Wow...this world is truly beautiful," I whispered to myself.

"Follow me, Kenji. Try to keep up." He took off flying.

I followed him closely. My wings looked so beautiful. The rich black became even richer and darker.

"Let's go faster. I can go faster!"

"Kenji, wait!"

I took off. I was flying so fast I could barely see what was around me. The wings felt so good. For the first time since I arrived, I smiled. Then before I could think, something hit my wings. Out of nowhere, I was falling from the sky. I looked around to see what I had hit. It was a girl. Her eyes were closed, and she was falling right beside me.

"*Hey!* Open your eyes!"

She didn't even flinch. I tried to move over to her and wake her, but it was no use. She had a broken arm. She continued to not respond to me. Now that I could see her up close, I realized she was so beautiful. Her brown skin, curly hair, and beautiful face left me speechless. I grabbed her and tried to carry her up, but we still kept falling. I looked back at my wings...They were broken. I wrapped my wings around her and pushed a little bit more power into them. While she was inside my wings, I touched her arm and made some of my power flow into her. This fixed her arm right away and woke her up. She screamed. We kept falling. The ground was getting closer, yet I could not fly because of my broken wings. I shot more power into them, and they started to heal, but it was a bit too late. I wrapped my wings tightly around her. One second later, my back hit directly onto concrete. My blood splashed everywhere.

"Are you okay?"

"Yes, I'm okay. I think I am."

She got up from my chest. She looked terrified and was trembling. Great, someone else who is scared of me, I thought.

"Are you okay?" she asked.

"What?" I was confused. "Are you not scared of me?"

"Why would I be scared of you? But enough of that. Let me get you to a doctor. Don't move."

"No, no. I'm fine." I stood up immediately.

My wings were back to normal, and all the wounds in my back vanished like they were never there.

"What? How did you do that? How did we not die from that fall? Especially me. It felt like I landed on a pile of the softest feathers in the whole world."

"Yeah, I covered you with these." I pointed at my wings.

"Oh, thank you so much! You saved my life! What is your name? I've never seen you around before. Are you familiar with this area?" The questions just kept coming.

"No problem. I'm Kenji, and yeah, I'm new around here. Just got here 'bout two days ago."

"Oh nice. Oh, I'm sorry, but I have to go do something. I'll see you around, I'm sure." She took off running.

"Wait! What is your…" She was already gone, and I didn't even know her name.

She was truly beautiful. She also didn't hate me and was not scared of me. She saw my tail, my wings, and the black aura that emerged from me, yet she wasn't scared. On the contrary, she asked if I was okay. Maybe she was different from the other people here. Maybe she didn't hate me.

"Kenji! I finally found you! You are a faster flier than me."

"Oh, I didn't even notice that you were that far behind." I laughed.

"Yeah, and I'm considered a fast flier."

"Ahahaha!"

"Why are you so red, Kenji? Did you get a kiss from a girl? Hahaha!"

"*What*! No, I did no such thing." I felt my face getting hot.

"Yeah, right…So why is your face so red?"

"Umm…"

"Come on. Let's go home. It's getting dark already, and you have school tomorrow."

That's right. Tomorrow is the day when I begin to study. Tomorrow I begin my path to saving my mother. Maybe she knows what I am and where all this power came from. If anyone knows it must be her, I thought.

We made it home, and Jiro was waiting for us.

"So how was it?"

"It was great! I'm really exhausted. I think I'm just gonna go to bed."

"Before that, Kenji, I just want you to know that every day after school, you will be training with me. As you know, I am in charge of you when you are here, at least for now, that is. I am also in charge of knowing that your power won't go out of control or that you won't kill someone. Though I don't think you would do such a thing, I'm sure you want to know the limits of your power as much as the people around you and my superiors want to know. So starting tomorrow, I will be your at-home trainer."

"Yeah, yeah. You're right. The people here fear and hate me even though they don't know me. It makes me happy that you don't think that way. I'm gonna go to bed, but I'll see you for training tomorrow."

I smiled and went upstairs to my room. I took off my clothes and got into the shower. As the warm water hit my face, my smile became smaller and smaller. A minute later, my smile was gone. I once again felt sad and hopeless. I felt the pressure from tomorrow. I started to think about how people would think of me, and it made me sick to my stomach. I got out of the shower as soon as I felt clean. I went directly to bed. For a second, I lay looking up at the light of my room.

"Good night, sir," a woman said and turned off my light.

Still, I looked up. Out of nowhere, my face became hot.

"Why is she in my head?" I whispered to myself.

That brown skin, the curly hair, and those beautiful eyes. They wouldn't leave my mind. Deep down, I knew I might be getting distracted, but I hoped that I would see her again. I spent even more time that night thinking about what I would say to her when I saw her again. Before I knew it, I was already asleep.

* * *

The next morning, I woke up and went straight to the shower.

"Focus, Kenji. Today is the day when everything begins." I felt my face and noticed that there wasn't a smile. I smacked my face.

"You got this, Kenji! You will do this! You must do this! Save your mother, and find out who you are!"

I headed downstairs where Jiro was waiting for me.

"Good morning! Your breakfast is on the table."

"Morning, Jiro. Thank you!" I sat down at the table and ate my breakfast.

The food was just as amazing as it was the first time I ate it. I finished eating quickly and headed outside.

"Are you ready to go, boy?" asked Jiro.

"Yes, I'm ready."

Jiro and I got into the car and headed over to the academy. I couldn't contain my excitement.

"Jiro, have they said anything about me?" I asked.

"What do you mean?"

"Like the people you work for. Are they afraid of me?"

"Oh, I see. I don't think you should focus on that at the moment. Just focus on what is in front of you for now. I'll deal with my superior."

"All right." I said as I felt the fear of not being accepted gripped tightly around my neck.

It was quiet for a moment. I looked out of the window and saw all the kids running and flying. Some of them were in cars just like I was.

"Okay, we are here. Have a great day, and try not to kill anyone."

"I won't."

I got out of the car and followed all the kids walking into the building. I was so amazed at the number of kids. There were even more than last time, and they were all different. I walked into the building. As soon as I walked in, I noticed how much louder it was. It was like everyone was having a different conversation with everyone else. I heard a sound coming from what seemed like the ceiling of the building. I looked around, and everyone was gone. Then I noticed that I didn't know where I was going. I looked around for a moment, but it was no use. I started to walk around, but it was no use. I was lost.

"Kenji? You should be in class right now. Are you causing trouble on your first day of school?" It was the headmaster.

"No, I'm not." I sighed. "I'm just lost. I'm not sure where my class is."

"Oh, that's okay. I'll take you there!"

I followed the headmaster for a couple of minutes, and we reached a big door. "Zero S" was written on the door.

"Here it is, Kenji."

"Thank you, headmaster!"

I walked through the door, and immediately all eyes were on me. I looked around, and I noticed that there weren't a lot of people in this class—only about twelve, including me.

"You must be the new guy. Come here, boy. Introduce yourself."

I walked in front of the class.

"My name is Kenji. I hope that we can be friends."

I'm not sure if that was too straightforward, but I chose the word *friend* because I didn't want them to fear me once they found out what was inside me.

"Go take a seat over there," said the teacher.

"Kenji!"

I looked up as I was walking to find a seat.

"Hey, over here, hero!"

It was her. The girl from yesterday was in my class. I walked over to her and sat right next to her.

"I didn't know you were in my class. Even though I should have guessed since you saved me from that fall"

"Oh, that was nothing special. We were both falling because of me so it was the least I could do."

We chatted for a couple of minutes before we started talking about powers.

"So...new transfer student, what is your power?" she asked.

"Well, you saw, didn't you?"

"All I saw were black wings. Which is a first for me."

"You are in my seat, boy," I heard a voice right above me say. " I think you should move."

I looked up. It was a guy. He looked furious for some reason.

"I said *move!*"

I sighed. Not wanting to cause trouble, I stood up. As I was standing up, the girl grabbed my arm. She looked so scared. I sat back down and looked up at him.

"I think I'll be sitting here from now on. Go find another seat. There are plenty of open seats over there." I pointed at a group of open seats at the front of the class.

"What did you say to me?"

"I said, I'm not moving!" I said confidently

"You're new here, so I'll show you how things work around here." He grabbed my head and started to squeeze it. "You must not know who I am. When I say move, you move!"

I noticed the teacher wasn't doing anything.

"Would you like to settle this somewhere else? I hate to break a classroom on my first day." I looked deep into his eyes. I could feel my power start to spill out of my body like an overflowing cup of water.

"Teacher?" said the boy. "We should have a class ranking again. Since we have a new student, he should know he is among the top class."

"Very well then. Disagreements are fixed through contests here, so he would only be fighting you. This also means that if you lose, he will take your spot as number two."

This was great. Number two would be a great spot for me. It was not at the top but close so people would have to accept me.

"That is fine by me. It's not like this little boy will beat me."

"Very well then. Class, follow me please."

Everyone got up and walked toward the door. The guy let go of my head and walked toward them as well.

"I shouldn't have grabbed your arm."

"No, this will actually work out in my favor."

"No, Kenji, you don't understand. He's number two!"

"That doesn't really mean anything to me."

"He is number two in the entire school. The second strongest. Only second to his older brother. He is a member of the God clan! They are the ones who rule over this world. I am number three, and I am nowhere near his level. Every time we fought, he humiliated me."

"Oh, I see." I smiled at her. "I still don't care. I don't care who he is or who his brother is. I don't care who his daddy is. He is standing in my way, and he hurts you. He must know his place."

We walked out of the classroom. Our class was waiting for us. We followed our teacher outside.

"Right here will be the match," said the teacher.

There was a big, open field right next to the school. It was full of white flowers.

"All right, everyone, back up. The two fighters, get ready."

The boy and I walked forward a bit.

"Start!" screamed the teacher.

"Listen, kid, my name is—"

"I don't care what your name is, man."

"You little—" he ran toward me.

Before I noticed, he punched me clean in the chest. The punch pushed me off my feet and sent me flying. I hit the floor seconds later and got up like nothing had happened.

"Now you will notice the power of a god!" he shouted.

"This kid is such a pain," I said to myself.

He ran toward me again, getting ready to kill me, it seemed.

"I am a *god*!" He threw another fist.

This time, I just moved out of the way. Then he threw another one and another one. None of them hit me.

"You know, for a god, you are awfully slow." I felt the darkness begin to spill from me. "I think it is time I show you what I can do." I walked right up to him and looked him right in the eye. I noticed that he was a bit taller than I was. I took my wings out and levitated a few feet above him. Now he was looking up at me.

"Sorry, I refuse to look up at someone who is inferior to me." The darkness took over once again

"What did you say?"

"I said, lower your head, boy!"

I swung my foot and connected with his face. He was knocked to the ground. Seconds later, I landed on the ground and looked at my leg. The skin on my leg was burned off.

"*Hahahaha!* You can't touch me, new guy. People who touch a god with the intent to hurt them will burn. What will you do now?"

My leg healed just seconds after. I walked right up to him.

"Lower your head." I gripped his face with my hand.

I felt the burning sensation go all the way up my arm. Still, I didn't care. He made me a bit angry. I jumped up and flew a couple of feet into the air, still gripping onto his face.

"Now you will know despair, boy," I said and dropped him.

I flew down and caught him before he hit the floor.

"I won't kill you," I said, and we landed on the ground.

He started to tremble in front of me and dropped to his knees.

"Hey, teach, I'm sure that is enough for your evaluation."

"Yes, yes, it is. All right, everyone, back to class."

Everyone followed the teacher back to class. They all looked disgusted by me.

"Is he a monster?"

"How did he beat a god?"

This was what I heard them say as they walked by—everyone except her. She ran toward me.

"Oh, Kenji, are you all right?" She grabbed my arm.

"You're going to be okay. I'm a member of the Phoenix clan." My arm was suddenly covered in flames.

"People call us gods, and we are…but that is not how we see ourselves. We are doctors who can cure anything. There is nothing that we cannot take care of."

I looked at my warm and realized that the flames weren't hot. They were warm. It felt like the sun gently kissing my arm on a cold winter night. I saw my arm heal even faster than when it heals on its own. Her help wasn't necessary seeing as my arm wasn't really hurt. But man did it feel nice.

Maybe I couldn't save my mom, but maybe *she* could!

"Hey, will I ever know your name?"

"Oh yeah, I guess I never told you?" She smiled at me. "My name is Amariah."

CHAPTER 5

I found it. I finally found a way to save my mother. She could be saved! I'd find out who I was, where I came from, where this power came from. We could save her. Amariah was the salvation I was looking for. She was my answer.

It had been a couple of days since the little entanglement with the number-two kid. Every day after that had been so boring. The only part I looked forward to was when I got to see her. School was not what I thought it was going to be. I learned more from training with Jiro at home than at school. Ever since I beat that number-two kid, people kept challenging me, but it was just so boring. They were all so weak. I really wanted to see what Number One was like, but he never showed up. At least I never saw him. Maybe I'd ask Amariah about him.

"It's time to go, Kenji," said Jiro.

"You know, I think I'll fly today!"

"You've come a long way. And your power just gets stronger every time we fight."

"Is that so? It sounds like you're getting soft on me. Maybe I should start calling you 'boy.'"

"Hahahah, not a chance!" Jiro placed his hand on my head and rubbed it.

"You still have a ways to go, kid. Now head on to school."

My black feathers came out, and a second later, I was flying on my way to school. I placed my hand on my head as I was flying.

"Urghhhh! Why does he have to do that where everyone in the house can see…so embarrassing!"

I made it to school, and there she was.

"Hey, Kenji. How was your weekend?"

"It was good. I have just been training."

We walked to class together. I couldn't help but notice that people were staring at us—and how much people here really didn't like me. All because they said I was a demon.

"It doesn't bother you, Amariah? The fact that they see you with me ?"

"No, not at all actually. I'm your friend, and that is between me and you. Besides they don't really know you; they just think they know. In reality, they don't at all. They just judge you because of the color of your wings."

"Yeah, they all think I am a monster."

"They should be thanking you. After you beat up that bully, he stopped picking on the weaker people around school. Also you should know there are those who hate you but also those who admire you."

"Is that right? Why don't they speak up?" I asked in frustration.

"I think they are waiting for you to beat Number One."

"I was thinking of doing that, but I do not know who that is."

"You will see him sooner or later." Her voice sounded worried.

We walked into class and noticed there was someone new sitting in front of the class.

"Well, look who decided to show up today. Our number-one ranked student." Said the teacher.

I looked at him and realized who he was. He was the guy in the middle. He was the guy who had attacked me when they were deciding which class I was going to be in. It was him. He was Number One?

"Hello, everyone! My name is Chintu, and I am the god of this world."

"What? Is what he is saying true? He is a god? Like the one above the others?" I asked Amariah.

"Yes. He is not just number one at this school. He is number one in the whole world. He is god among the gods and the strongest being that ever lived. I heard rumors that he has never been hurt in a fight before."

"Well, that rumor is false. He's been hurt by me."

"That is right," said Chintu.

"So to think you are a god!"

"Oh no, Kenji. I know that I am one. There is no god in this world that is even capable of hurting me; therefore, I am a god. A better god than they could ever be."

"Oh, what does that make me? You were hurt by my blood! You were hurt by me without me even attacking. I still remember how loud you were screaming."

Chintu's expression changed. His cocky smile vanished, and he now looked serious.

"So what do you wish to do, Kenji? Shall we fight to see who is the real god?"

I looked around for a second and noticed that everyone was on his side.

"Are you, this world's god, challenging me? Most people think I am a demon, but I think you believe I am the devil."

"Yes, Kenji! I do believe you are the devil. And the reality is that I can't wait to get rid of you!" Chintu had a sinister grin across his face.

"Wow, so scary, Chintu! Do you want to kill me?" I stared directly into his eyes.

"Listen, Kenji. Your darkness is nothing compared to the power I possess. My light will shine so bright that there will be no room for your shadows or darkness." His voice grew confident.

"Listen, Chintu! I came here to find a way to save my mother. But you just attacked me without even knowing who I was. I do not wish to take your throne. You can be god. I just wish to find out who I am."

"And what if you find out that you are the devil?" Everyone's eyes turned to me.

"Well, then the Devil I will be."

"If this actually comes to pass, I shall have your head, Kenji! You do not know what the demons did to us when they were alive."

"I have a question for you, Chintu. Are you afraid? You talk about how demons did such bad things in the past and how you will kill me because I too am a demon. But why don't you just kill me right now?"

Chintu became flustered.

"You were going on and on about how you were number one and how no one can hurt you…but I did! So I'll ask once again. Are you afraid? Maybe you put me in the highest-ranked class just to hide how scared you really are. Or maybe I'm missing something?"

"Huh—" Chintu stood up. "We will meet, Kenji! And when we do, you will experience the sorrow I felt when your kind took what I loved most from me."

Chintu walked out of the classroom. I noticed that in the middle of talking, I had gotten up and walked toward him. After he left, I walked back to my seat next to Amariah.

"Wow, you are brave!" said Amariah.

"What do you mean?"

"To talk to him in the way you did is either brave or crazy."

"What was his problem anyway?"

"Well, Chintu, is a member of the Pure Light clan. It's said that the Pure Light race was the first race to ever be born. For a long time, they shone and gave life to the other races. That was until they ran into the demons."

"What happened after that?" I asked.

"Well, being total opposites created conflict, and the struggle for power started. In the end, the light won but at a cost. The only survivor was Chintu. The rest were killed by the demon race. It's said that his family was killed by just one demon. They were all murdered right in front of him. It is for that reason that not only he but a lot of people hate demons. When the light won the Battle over the World, the demons were cast to the underworld…but you already knew that. The only reason he is still in school is because after the war it took him a while to go back to being himself. Plus, even longer to get back into school. Still he is only a bit older than us, Kenji."

"So that is why he is so angry! Still I don't want power nor to do any harm, I just want to cure my mom. That is the only reason I came here in the first place."

"What happened to your mother?"

"She is in a paralyzed state. There seems to be nothing wrong with her physical body."

"So what is wrong then?"

"Well, she used her power to save me when I was still young. She was basically brought back to life. This had its side effects. I think it caused permanent damage to her brain. The brain is too complicated for me to fix. If it was just a broken arm, I could fix it, no problem."

"Oh, I see."

"Yeah, the reality is that I want to ask you if you could teach me how to cure something like that. I know that is selfish, but please, I need your help. There is no one else I can turn to. Everyone else *hates* me. So, please, would you teach me how to help her? I'll do anything!"

"Of course I'll help you. You saved my life after all."

"Thank you!"

* * *

It had been days since Amariah agreed to help me. Ever since that day, she had been coming over to my house every weekend to teach me everything she learned from the Phoenix family. We also became friendlier than before. Still…I'd yet to learn how to fix anything other than physical problems. Every time she brought a dead animal or something that was brain dead for me to fix, I never ended up fixing it. That day, she said she would bring a dog.

"Hey, Kenji!"

"Hey, Amariah! You're looking lovely as usual."

"Oh, thank you! If I didn't know any better, I would think you are flirting with me!" She smiled

"Hahaha, maybe I am!"

We talked for some time and had something to eat. The food tasted so much better when she was there. Sometimes, I would catch myself looking at her and have to remind myself to focus on the task I set out to do in the first place. It was like when she was around, the dark thoughts that filled my head just went away. It was almost as if I was actually happy. We finished eating and headed to the back yard.

"All right, Kenji, are you ready?" Said Amariah.

"Yes, let's do it!"

"All right, now, listen: this dog is dead. His brain no longer functions. Therefore, this dog is the perfect body to practice on. Since this dog was a living being, if you can't bring it back or at least bring back some form of brain activity in him, it is safe to assume that you just don't have the powers to save your mother."

"Oh, I see. Are you sure?"

"Yes, this dog was living once, but it got hit in the head. Eventually, it slowly died because its brain could not keep up with the damage."

I felt like I was under a lot of pressure. This dog would tell me if I had the power to save my mom or if I had to find another way. Still, I doubted that anyone would be willing to help me. So this was the only way.

"Okay, Kenji, are you ready?"

"Yes."

"All right, start!"

I placed my hand on the dog and started to push power into him slowly, making sure I had a clear picture in my mind of what I wanted the dog to look like. I saw the dog's body start to heal. Everything was going just as planned. I started to push more power, and it was healing even faster than before.

"I'm doing it, Amariah!"

"No, not yet. You just fixed the physical things. He is still unable to walk or move. It is not alive yet."

I started pouring even more power into the dog. Yet the dog would not move or breathe. So I threw more and more power into him, still trying not to give the dog more power than his body could handle, but the dog would not open his eyes. My head filled with frustration and anger. Suddenly, I noticed that my veins were almost popping out of my arms. I saw the darkness moving in my veins. It was flowing down to my hands and into the dog. Still, the dog stayed dead. I poured even more power into him. I screamed as my arms became dark from the power flowing to my hands.

"Kenji, stop!"

"No, not yet!"

I screamed, as I couldn't take the pain from my arms. Suddenly one of my veins burst. My blood looked so dark. All of the blood dripped onto the dog and into the mouth of the dog. Seconds later, my arm healed. I was disappointed in myself. Hated myself for coming up short. After all, the dog didn't move.

"Kenji, are you okay?"

Tears fell from my eyes. My eyes locked with Amariah's, and I just could not hold them back. For the first time ever, I was unable to keep my composure in front of someone. I felt so weak and hopeless and could not hold back the tears.

"Kenji, behind you!"

I looked back and noticed the dog was no longer lying down. He was standing and looking directly at me. His fur pitched black. His teeth grew abnormally. He looked angry and much bigger than he did before. He was still growing. I was now looking up at the dog. It was almost as big as the entire back yard.

"I did it!" I smiled

"No, Kenji. That dog is not alive. His body is just full of darkness. He probably doesn't even know what he is doing right now. The dog is still dead."

"How do you know?"

"Look at him, Kenji! This dog used to be so kind. He loved me. But now he wants to attack us. Look at him, Kenji." Amariah's lips tremble.

At that moment, I realized that I had created a monster. This poor animal couldn't rest in peace. Once again, tears filled my eyes. This was just one of the reasons these people hated me.

"Maybe...Chintu was right." I whispered

I walked toward the dog. He looked angry and started barking at me. Still I walked toward him. I took my wing out. I felt anger and rage, and deep down, I was disappointed in myself. I couldn't control my power any longer. My power began to pour out of my body. Suddenly the deep blue sky became dark, as dark as the darkest of nights. I flew up to the face of the dog. With no hesitation, the dog bit my lower half. I found myself stuck between his jaws. I felt my blood drip down my legs. I felt his teeth dig deep into my legs and abdomen. Yet I felt no pain. I placed my hand on the dog's nose. I felt him tremble. I felt his pain. I felt sorry for this animal. When I put my hand on his nose, I felt the darkness within him.

"I'm truly sorry, friend. I didn't mean to hurt you."

I started to suck the darkness in him back into my body. Slowly, he began to get smaller. I felt his body start to decompose as I took my power back. Before I knew it, he was back to his original size and then smaller until he eventually vanished. There wasn't a single trace of him. No ashes or fur, nothing. It was as if I had consumed him.

"Aaahhh!" I screamed.

"Kenji, I'm so sorry it had to be this way."

"I can't save her. No matter how hard I try, I can't save her. I don't have the power to restore complex things. If I even try, I'll just end up turning her into a monster. That is all I am: a monster!"

Dark clouds now covered the sky. I lifted my arm in the air and then swung it back down. This created an enormous amount of wind. This wind parted the sky. Seconds later, the sun was shining once again, like nothing ever happened.

"Kenji…are you okay?" She fell to her knees and her body trembled in fear as she gazed up at me.

I don't know what I am anymore.

"Yeah, I'm fine."

This was a day that I wished to forget. I created a monster and later killed it. I erased it from existence. That poor animal. I put him through so much.

"Amariah…will I be able to help my mother?"

"Kenji…I don't believe you will be able to, Kenji. The dog is dead. Yet, you just somehow made his body move out of pure will. Still the dog was never aware. I'm sorry, Kenji."

"I see." I looked up at the sky and closed my eyes briefly.

As I stood on the ground, I felt my legs turn to jelly. It felt as if a part of me died alongside that animal..

"After all this, after all this darkness, I am still not good enough."

"No, you are a great person, Kenji."

"Kenji!" It was Jiro.

"Jiro, you saw what happened?"

"Yes, I did. That was the power the demons used years ago to try to take over. They used dead bodies and made those bodies fight for them. There weren't many demons, yet their army of dead was enormous. The dead were fairly weak because their bodies were decomposing. With that being said, that dog wasn't weak at all. If anything, he became a thousand times stronger, and he was alive."

"Yeah! That's why I felt scared," said Amariah.

"Kenji! You must never show this to anyone. If you do, the gods will come after you. They will not rest until they see the end of you."

"Am I really a monster?" My heart felt cold.

"No, but those who had your power before you were. Amariah, make sure you take what happened to the grave. If you want to see Kenji again, then you will tell no one."

"I won't tell anyone," said Amariah.

"With that being said, why don't we go inside and eat something?"

CHAPTER 6

It had been days since I created the monster. Now I was yet again lying down, staring at the ceiling of the room, thinking of what there was left for me to do. I found myself lost yet again. All this power and I couldn't even use it to save the people who meant a lot to me. Again, I didn't know what my next move would be. Still I knew I must move forward.

I got out of my bed and got ready for school. As I flew to school, I noticed that everyone was looking at me—even more than usual. I landed on the ground. Everyone stared and kept their distance from me.

"Kenji!"

"Jiro? What are you doing here?"

"Kenji…they know. Someone saw you. They saw the dog. Chintu and the other gods said they are on their way to kill your mother."

"What? Why my mother? What did she do?"

"They are saying that you got your power from her! They believe that since the last demon fell to the underworld, you must have gotten your power from them. Plus, Chintu said that your drive to save your mother was here trying to obtain her power again. So even though you might be pure at heart, she could be one of the demons who killed others in the past."

"How did they know?" My body trembles.

"It was my brother. Ichiro works for Chintu. He must have wanted the information and my brother is just not strong enough to resist him. It doesn't matter now. If there is a chance, they will end her." his voice quaver.

"I'm going to save her. I'm going to the underworld."

"Kenji, they don't really care if your mother is or was or will be a good person. The real reason why they are going over there is to kill her. If there is a chance that she is a demon, they will end her. Then they will come after you, just because you guys are demons. That is the real reason."

"So why don't they just come after me? I am already here!"

"The real reason is that Chintu hates you. He wants you to feel the same pain he felt when he lost his parents."

"They had no idea who my mother was or whether she did or did not kill those people. They are going to kill her without even knowing if she really is dangerous. She is going to die because of me." I was filled with rage.

"Kenji, I have something for you. Take this sword. This sword seals inside of it the soul of all those who are cut by it. Still, You must be careful. This sword was originally made to kill demons. If you are cut by it, I don't think your powers will be able to save you. If it comes down to it and there is no other choice…use it!"

We made my way to the stairs of despair. There I was surprised by Amariah.

"What are you doing here?" I asked.

"Kenji, ever since you stood up for me against that bully, my life was never the same. So ever since that day, I have been trying to repay you for setting me free. I want to help you be free. So I tried to help you save your mother, but I failed."

"You don't have to help me do anything. If I'm being real with you, the real reason I helped you was because I thought you were beautiful."

Suddenly Amariah began to act shy. Still her beautiful brown skin shone with the sun's kiss. Her smile made me feel calmer and think a bit more clearly.

"Hey, listen, I'm going down there to save my mother."

"I know. That is why I am here. You set me free, so I will stick by your side."

"Amariah, you could die down there. I don't think that I could live in a world without you."

"I'm going!"

"Ugh…This is no time to play around."

"Kenji! I'm going."

"Fine. Here, take this."

"How do you have this? This is one of the swords used by the gods to seal and kill beings who try to take over the world."

"I gave it to him," Jiro answered.

"Oh, I see."

"All right, let's get moving."

We made our way down the stairs. Suddenly, I noticed that I was becoming angrier, and the calm slowly drifted away from me.

"Amariah, if I lose control down there, use the *sword* on me."

"I will not do such a thing." she cried

"Listen, we don't even know how many of them there are. We don't know how capable they are. So I will be going all out. If I lose control, use the sword."

"Ken—"

"I'm not playing!" I shouted.

"Fine, but only as a last resort."

We kept going down the stairs for a while. The closer I got, the more I felt myself succumbing to the darkness. It was as if it were leaking from my forehead. I placed my hand on my forehead and felt something long, curvy, and pointy growing right above my eyebrows.

"Kenji, you have horns now?" asked Amariah.

"Yes, it appears that my powers keep growing and at a faster rate than before. I don't know how much of this power I can control. That is why you have the sword."

"We are here," said Jiro.

Before us was the underworld—the place where there was no good or evil, happiness or sorrow. All you could see and feel in this place was pain and suffering. People were fighting for their lives every day, wondering if there was even a reason to live.

For a second, I looked at Amariah. Her expression was one of shock, fear, and terror.

"Kenji…what is this place?" Amariah asked me.

"This…this is my home!"

"Home? This place is your home? It's hard to breathe here!" She began to sweat.

"Yeah, the air is pretty dense here."

I let Amariah take a second to adjust to the atmosphere in the underworld. Suddenly, we heard people screaming. We ran toward the screams. The screams were getting louder. We realized that it wasn't just one person. Everyone was screaming.

"What the hell is happening here?" I shouted.

"Kenji! Kenji, is that you?" someone shouted back.

"Who's there?"

"Kenji, help me!"

I saw a man lying on the ground. It looked like parts of a building had fallen on top of him. I ran to him. When I got closer, I started to recognize his face more. I ran faster and faster. It was my father. I flew to him as fast as I could.

"I'm gonna get you out." I cried

With one big flap of my wings, I pushed the rocks back. His body was fully exposed.

"What happened to you?" I asked.

"I came to town to buy food for your mother and I. They descended from above. They came for your mother. I tried to stop them, but I was too weak. He said his name was Chintu," said father as tears rushed down his face.

My blood boiled. When I took a closer look at my father, I noticed that he had lost a lot of blood. The lower half of his body was completely crushed.

"Amariah, please help him!"

"Kenji…I can't. He's lost too much blood. Even if I fixed his legs, there is no way that he would survive."

"Please, Amariah, you have to try…He is the only one who has been there for me. He took care of me. Even now, the reason he is like this is because of me."

"I'm so, so sorry, Kenji, but if I try to bring him back, all he will feel is pain, and still he will die. I can't help him anymore." I saw tears fall from her eyes.

"Listen to me, Son. My time has come. We all must go one day, and it just happens that this is my time. You can still go help your mother. Your wings are even darker than hers on the day she saved you. That is how I know there will be no one who will have greater strength than yours. Remember to use your darkness, and don't let the darkness use you." His hand gently wiped away the tears from my face.

"No, please stay with me!"

I witnessed my father's eyes slowly closing as he lay in my arms. I placed my hand on his chest. I felt his heart. It quickly faded. So many thoughts filled my head. But the only way was for me to give him some of my power. My hands trembled. What if he turns into a monster? That was the thought that came to my mind.

I was scared. I felt like my chest was so heavy.

"Listen to me please!" My father spoke. "You have your own battle to fight now. Look at you…You have been gone for a long time, and you have grown so much. You made friends and became stronger. Now it is time to use that power to find who you are. It is a lonely road ahead of you. At times, it will feel like there is no one there for you. But know that I will be rooting for you on the other side. I know it is time for me to go, but I'm happy to know that my son will be okay here in the underworld or in the world above. I love you, and I will be watching over you."

My father's heart stopped beating. For a long moment, everything was silent. I couldn't breathe. I couldn't see. Everything went dark.

"Hey there, boy…" There was a voice coming from within me.

"Who are you?" I asked.

"I am you. Well, at least the darker, angrier, stronger version of you. I am the better you," he told me.

"The better me? Why are you here?"

"Well, your spirit has always been strong, even as a child when Mother saved us. I've just been waiting for a little crack in your armor so I can slip right out. And lately your armor has been breaking. Hahahaha, are you stressing, little guy?"

"Listen, you don't know me!"

"Oh, but I do. I've been here the entire time. We were born together, and we will die together. We are one, we have always been one, and we will always be one. Look around you. We are talking inside of your head…inside of my head."

"How come I never knew of you?"

"Because I am the darkness deep inside you. Mother told me that I had to be sealed deep in your heart so that we never hurt anyone. She said something about how her darkness took over her in the past, causing her to do things she didn't like or want to do."

"The darkness took over her?"

"Yes, her armor was completely broken, and Mother and her inner self did not get along. That is why the darkness took control of her."

"So what exactly are you?" I asked.

"I am you!"

"I never knew of you!"

"Actually, you have always known about me. You just always pushed me back. Every time you get angry and more power just comes out of nowhere, that is me. You just never accepted me."

"What if I let you in? Will I become what she hated to be? Will I hurt people like she did?"

"No, we won't do that! I don't want to take over your body. I just want to be one with you. Look around." His voice sounded desperate.

I took a look around and noticed how dark this place was. There was no life. It was very cold, and he was all alone here.

"You were all alone here?" I asked

"Yeah, I've been here since we were kids. Never seen the outside world. I could hear you...laughing, getting angry, crying. I have listened to it all."

"Listen, after all of this, I will come back for you!" I said.

"No, please do not leave me here. I feel trapped. I told you that I don't want your body. I'm not going to take over you; I just want to be free alongside you!" he shouted.

"You know what is going on out there. Chintu will kill Mother. My mother, your mother, our mother," I insisted.

"Please...don't leave me here all alone again."

"I am so sorry!" Tears fell from my eyes.

"Please! Look at you: you have the wings already and one horn. I have the other one, and your wings would just get bigger and darker. Nothing will change. Just please let me out."

"I will come back for you. I promise!" I closed my eyes.

"Please, come back soon. I'm all alone here."

As I closed my eyes, I realized that the other me was just a child version of me. I opened my eyes and saw my father. I no longer felt his heartbeat in my hand. He was dead. There was no life left in him. As I stared at his face, I noticed a water drop fall on his cheek. I touched my face with my bloodstained hands. The water was coming from me. It was coming from my eyes.

I was crying. I could hear the screams and the sounds of people's homes collapsing. I felt no emotion. I felt no pain. Yet tears still continued to form in my eyes and fall onto my dead father's face. I had no words and didn't know how to feel. Everything felt like it was collapsing on me, like a glass full of water ready to spill.

"Kenji...I'm so sorry," said Amariah.

"Why?" I asked.

"Huh?"

"Why are you sorry? You had nothing to do with this. But him...I will kill him. Chintu...I will have his head."

Jiro and Amariah looked at me, scared of the monster that I had become.

"Have the sword in hand, Amariah. I'm not sure how I will handle what happens next."

"Kenji, please control yourself. You are scaring us!" Amariah cried.

As I tried to calm down, I could hear Jiro tell Amariah that my power had surpassed his. I already knew that this was the case. Ever since I talked to my inner self, I noticed my power kept growing stronger. Sooner or later, the other Kenji would come out. I could feel myself burning from the inside out. Somehow I just knew that I would end up losing control.

"Sorry, I'm still in control for now. Keep the sword ready. You know, just in case," I said to Amariah.

"I'm sorry about your father, Kenji. There was nothing we could have done; we were too late," said Jiro.

"Don't be sorry. This was not your doing. There is nothing you could have done. If anything, I should take the time to finally thank you for being a father figure for me when I left to come to the world above. I wouldn't be here today if it wasn't for you, so thank you, Jiro." Tears continued to fall from my eyes.

I formed a small ball of dark power in my hand. It was about the size of a grain of rice. I then threw it on the ground next to my father. The small ball made a hole big enough for my father to fit in. I gently picked him up and placed him in the hole. I slowly picked up the dirt from around the hole, and with my own hand, I placed it on top of my father. Before long, his entire body was covered. I thankfully took the smallest feather from my wings. My wings were now so large that this feather was the size of a tombstone. I placed the feather on top of the dirt. I tried to hold back the tears, but it was no use. At the end of the day, I was just a kid.

I closed my eyes.

"Hey, other me. How are you?"

"You came back! I'm crying too. You know he was my dad too! I never even got to see him."

"Yeah, I know." I walked up to the other version of me.

I hugged him. I felt his pain and suffering. At that moment, I realized all of my emotions were just pushed down really far, and this other half of me was holding on to them.

"Come...Let's say our last goodbye to Father, okay?" I held this version of me by the hand.

"Wait...You're going to let me out?" He asked.

"Yes, I will." I smiled

"Are you sure?" I felt his hand start to tremble.

"Yeah, from now on, we will be one. How it always should have been!" I reached down to hug him.

We hugged even tighter and slowly became one person. After that, I opened my eyes and felt the other half of me.

"Hey, can you see?"

"Yeah, I can."

"Okay, one last goodbye..." I felt us both starting to become emotional.

Our legs trembled as we took a step closer to where our father was. I could feel our lips shake. I felt us cry.

"We love you, Dad."

CHAPTER 7

Living and dying are both a part of being human, right? If that is the case, what is the point of living if you are just going to die? All intelligent creatures are the same. They are all selfish in some way. They fight for what they want—even if what they think is right causes harm to someone else. They are all driven by emotions. Love and fear are the most influential of these emotions. People kill for those they love. Those who live in fear would do anything for some type of safety. Selfish creatures only care about themselves. Still…in the end, I am one of those beings, and right then, the emotion that was pushing me forward was anger. We wanted *blood*.

After I said goodbye to Father for the last time and became one with the inner me, Jiro, Amariah, my inner self and I kept moving forward. We knew how hard the battle in front of us was going to be. Still we kept moving on. I don't know why these two were helping me, but I was glad that they were there. We rushed up the mountain to my home. That was where Mother was. As we reached the top of the mountain, I could see a beam of light coming from the sky. It was Chintu. That light I saw was a dagger. He was flying in the air pointing the light dagger at my mother.

"No, I can't lose her too!" I shouted.

I rushed to get in front of my mother as fast as a cloud. Just when I was about to reach her, I was stopped by the people who came with Chintu.

"You must go on, Kenji. I will hold these guys back. You go save your mother. This is a thank-you for helping me open my eyes about the truth of the world we live in," said Jiro.

"Thank you," we said as we kept moving forward.

"I'll come with you, Kenji!" said Amariah.

I took off flying as fast as I could. I saw Chintu throw the dagger at Mother. The dagger became smaller and smaller the closer it got to her. It got to a point where it was just as wide as the palm of my hand. I flew as fast as I could, trying to somehow get in front of it.

"It's too far. I won't make it."

"Yes, we will. You have me now, Kenji. We are one. We will make it."

"You're right!"

I put all of my strength into my wings and pushed as hard as I could. The light got closer and closer to her eyes. I reached out my hand, trying to at least get my hand in front of the dagger. I stretched my hand out, placing the back of my hand on Mother's forehead. At the same time, the dagger hit my palm. My palm began to burn. It felt like my hand was melting slowly. It was making a hole through my hand. I saw my skin slowly melting away. Before it could go all the way through my hand, I pushed it back. I tried to push and push back, but it wouldn't move an inch.

"Push it, Kenji!" screamed the other part of me.

I pushed and pushed and pushed. Eventually, I pushed the dagger back just enough to where I could fit my other hand behind it. I flushed the darkness into my hand and pushed back even harder. I felt an excruciating pain coming from the front of my hand. The dagger had completely gone through it. Using the hole in my hand, I grabbed the dagger with all my strength and sent it back to Chintu. Chintu stopped the dagger as if it were nothing. I looked at my hand. It was completely burned off. Blood gushed out of my forearm. A deep pool of blood formed at my feet. With my other hand, I picked up as much blood as I could. I threw it at him, hoping to burn him. The blood flew up, but only one drop of it reached him.

"*Aahhh!* How dare you throw your disgusting blood at me!" Chintu's arm burned.

He then took the dagger and compressed it down to something even smaller. It now looked like a nail.

"I will kill her, and then I will kill you!" Chintu shouted.

The nail traveled faster than anything I had ever seen before. My hand wasn't healed all the way. The nail was coming straight for Mother's head. I placed my hand in front of it once more. I pushed power down my hand to try to stop it once again. This time, I was too late. Late once again. I looked at my hand, and there was a hole going right through it. I turned around. Everything went silent. I saw Mother's chin resting on her chest. Blood dripped down her forehead. I looked back at my hand, and it was just like that day, the day I left everything behind. I wondered if any of this would have happened if I had just stayed quiet. It was not like I had learned much of anything.

I slowly walked toward my mother. My hands went back to normal. Like nothing ever happened. They were healed. I kneel down next to her. As I looked up at her, I saw the hole in her head. The nail had gone straight through her head. I placed my head on her chest. I heard nothing. Her heart no longer beat. Anger filled my mind.

"You will die for this."

I let the darkness take full control of me. I no longer held back. I no longer tried to fight whatever was deep inside of me. It was like both sides of me agreed to just let it happen. I felt my wings grow much larger, so much that it felt as if my bones were being broken apart to make room. I felt horns growing out of my head. Now it wasn't just one. There were two, and they were bigger. It felt like my skull was being pounded in between two rocks over and over. I placed my hand on my head and shouted in pain. I then felt my hands become wet. I opened my eyes. It was blood. Blood was flowing out of my eyes like tears. I looked at my hands and arms, and I could see the darkness spread throughout my body like it was running through my veins. I felt true darkness, like it had always been a part of me. This pain, the feeling of the darkness ripping through my veins. My muscles were moving around and tearing apart. My wings doubled in size. All that pain felt good. It felt so good. It was a feeling that I had never felt before. I felt power. It was like nothing could stop me. It was as if this pain killed the gentle side of me. Now all that was left was the thirst for blood.

I stared up at Chintu. I flew right into his face so fast that I surprised myself. I was now face to face with him. His eyes moved frantically. I felt my aura consume him.

"Is that fear I see in your eyes?" I grabbed his jaw with my right hand.

I squeezed and squeezed. I could see his jaw bones cracking. As I let go of his jaw, I slowly descended to the ground. We stared into each other's eyes. Before even saying a word, Chintu hurried to the ground. I went after him.

"Are you running from me?" I asked as he faced away from me.

"Oh no. I would never run from my inferiors."

"Inferior? I don't think you understand the situation you are in!"

"I will show you real power, kid."

Slowly I saw white wings emerge from Chintu, just like mine did from me. His wings were the opposite of mine, such a clear white, so pure.

"So you are just like me?" I asked.

"No, you are the darkness of this world, and I am the light. We are two sides of a coin!"

"So what are you?"

"I am an angel. A being who is all pure. Not tainted by the ugliness of the living world."

"The ugliness that you created?"

"I did not do this. I did not make the world like this."

"So who did?"

For a moment, he was silent, as if he had nothing to say.

"You. You and your kind did this. Everyone would have been happy if your mother hadn't killed my parents, my people...the protectors of this world."

"Listen, Chintu. I'm sorry that this happened to you. But that was long ago. Why can't we just work together to make this world better?"

"It is too late for that. Look around you. This world is already too far gone. I will destroy it. Then I will rebuild it. This world will be perfect."

"That is impossible. As long as there is good, there will be bad. As long as there is a winner, someone will lose. There will always be jealousy and envy. That's reality. It does not matter what your intent is."

"I guess there is only one way we'll find out."

"I will not let you do this. I want to find out who I am, and for that, I need this world. I tried to be sympathetic with you. But you have gone too far. You have taken everything from me—my father, my mother, and now you plan on taking this world from me! I will make sure that today you take your last breath."

I'd lost control. I was no longer me. My vision went black.

"Kenji, you have to fight it. We have to fight it!"

"It's too late for us. He took everything. We have nothing left!"

"Right."

I felt both sides of me give in. I fell into the darkness. We gave in. There was nothing else to fight for. So if I die here, then that's that, I thought. I knew I was one with the darkness. I became the thing they all judged me for. My teeth became sharper. My skin darkened. My eyes became as dark as my wings. I felt nothing. It was as if I was experiencing my life in third person. I was no longer in control.

Suddenly, my body shouted, and a beam of dark light shot toward Chintu. He flew upward to move out of the way. My body instantly followed him. Everything around me moved so slowly—everything but Chintu and myself. I threw balls of darkness at Chintu, but none of them hit. We were moving so fast I couldn't make out anything around me but him. He threw light back at me. As it hit the balls of darkness, loud bangs shocked everyone around us. I stopped and looked around. Everyone had stopped fighting. I looked up. The clash of our power had broken the ceiling of the underworld. There was a gigantic hole. The people from the world above could now see the underworld. They could see me—the monster they had created. Chintu flew right at me. His fist pushed against my face. Suddenly I was sent flying. After a second, my body hit the ground. Before I could get back up, I felt Chintu land on top of me. He hit my face. Again and again and again. I felt blood drip down my head. Chintu's fist kept repeatedly punching down on me. I felt nothing. I grabbed his arm. I looked at my hand. My nails grew. I shaped my hand like a claw. With all my strength, I pushed it against his chest. My nails sank right in like his body was liquid. My palm followed right after. My hand gripped his flesh. It had gone completely through his body. I let go of his arm. Chintu took a couple of steps back. My arm slid out of his chest. Chintu hit the floor. Blood coming out of his mouth. His skin looked pale. I threw his flesh back at him. I stood up and looked deep into his eyes. He was lifeless.

I walked toward my mother. The last hope I had to find out what I really was was gone for good. I created a hole just like I had for my father. I placed her in it and placed the dirt on top. I took one of my feathers and placed it on top.

I took a long look around. Jiro was on the floor, and so were the people who tried to stop me. Amariah was looking at me with the sword in her hands. I knew she must be scared. I didn't blame her. If I saw myself through her eyes, what would I see? A demon? A monster? A hero? Or a villain? It didn't matter anymore. She was ready to end me. To end this monster that I had become. I didn't blame her.

As I kept looking around, I noticed that the eyes of the people in the underworld were fixed on the hole. They noticed the light from the sun. It was like the light that would guide you to heaven. As I looked up, I noticed that the people from above were looking down at the people from the underworld. They looked so scared, as if they were looking down at hell.

I coughed. Blood gushed out of my mouth.

I looked down. There was a yellow light going through me. As the light vanished, I turned around. It was Chintu. He was alive. The hole in his chest was slowly closing.

"How are you alive?"

"I am an angel, Kenji. I cannot die from something as simple as that!"

"But...I saw you. You were dead on the floor."

"I would never die before fixing this world."

I looked down at my body. Blood dripped down. Slowly I began to rock back and forth. My body drifted backward as I slowly lay on the dirt. I looked up at the hole and the light that came from it.

My eyes slowly closed, my mind drifted away, and my body rested on the pool of blood. I didn't feel, see, or smell anything. Complete numbness.

Is this how I go out? I wondered.

If I died here, what was the purpose of all of this? What was the purpose of leaving home? The purpose of trying to find myself? What is all meaningless? Was it all for nothing?

Negative thoughts filled my head. I opened my eyes. It didn't matter if it had meaning or not. The world did not deserve to pay for our mistake. I would end it all now. I stood up. My stomach was closing incredibly slowly. At this rate, I would lose too much blood and die.

"So...you're still alive, I see."

"You won't kill me before I kill you!"

Chintu and I rushed at each other. We exchanged blows, spilling our blood all over the underworld, destroying anything and everything in our path. With every clash of our fists, the world around us trembled. Everything crumbled around us. While flying in the air, Chintu and I grabbed onto each other's wings. We started to rip them apart. Black and white feathers fell from the sky. Both worlds stood still and watched us monsters kill each other. Exhausted, we both landed.

"Give up already, Kenji. Your death is already certain."

"No, you will come with me. We will meet our creator together. We will ask him the reason for our existence."

"Even on your deathbed, you still stand in my way."

I picked up some of the blood that was flowing out of my stomach. I dashed toward Chintu and rubbed it into his eyes.

"*Aaahhh*, you bastard!"

Before he had time to move away, I took my hand and pierced his chest. I dragged my hand through his body trying to find where his heart was.

"I found it!" I grinned.

I dragged my nails into his heart.

"What are you doing, Kenji?" he asked as his body became paralyzed.

I let the darkness seep into his heart, slowly consuming him from the inside.

I stepped away, and the hole in his chest closed, not letting the darkness escape. His pure white wings became a dirty black, a disgusting color. His aura was no longer the bright-white color it had been. It was now a shade of dirty gray. His skin became similar to mine.

"What have you done to me?"

"If you cannot die as an angel, then I will kill you as a demon!"

I grabbed him by the arms and started spinning in circles. Before too long, I slammed him into the dirt.

I coughed and placed my hand over my mouth.

My blood…it was black. I ran over to Amariah. She was trembling at the sight of me.

"Amariah, I need your help."

"Kenji, I can't save you. I don't have the power. I-I don't have that much power in me."

"Please, I need you to try. Before he wakes up."

I dropped to the floor. Amariah stood over me. I felt her power surround my body. I was so warm. It was like a blanket in the cold, long winter. I could see Amariah trying her hardest. On her back, I saw small, fiery wings. I could feel her power in me.

It wasn't enough. The hole in my body wouldn't close. There was almost no blood left in me.

"Kenji, I am so sorry!" Amariah cried.

"There is no reason to cry. Before even getting to this point, somehow, I knew that it would come to this." I stood up, blood dripping down my body.

"Use the sword on us! It is the only way."

"Kenji, I won't kill you!"

"I'm already dying, Amariah. Chintu wants to kill almost everyone in this world. So don't think about it as if you are killing me. It's more like you are saving yourself and all other living things along with you. Maybe they'll even give you a statue for saving the world." I laughed.

"Kenji…"

"Let's go! There is no time."

I walked toward Chintu. Amariah followed me.

"A demon and a phoenix working together. I thought I would never see the day!" Chintu cried.

"She is not helping. Just watching!"

We rushed at each other. Blow for blow, we fought, destroying anything that was around us. The shock from our powers clashing knocked Amariah back. My goal was just to get him close enough to her so that the sword would kill him. Since he was a demon now, it should work. My power was flowing through him.

There was no need to hold back. I let the darkness take over me once again.

Blow after blow, I knocked Chintu down. At the same time, I felt my life slowly drain from me. Everything suddenly became ominous. It was clear to me that there was only one way for everything to end.

In the middle of the fight, I glanced over at Amariah. Immediately, she drew the sword. With a single punch, Chintu spiked me to the ground.

"You are getting distracted by the phoenix. You should never look away when fighting me. By the way, I should thank you for the extra power you were kind enough to give me." Chintu's voice became cocky

"So the angel has come to the dark side?"

"No, Kenji. My priorities have changed. I will destroy this world and everyone with it. Then I will rebuild it, to something better. Killing you in the process."

I got up and faced Chintu. I opened my arms.

"Come get m—"

Before I could finish, Chintu's arm went right through my heart. Suddenly it got heavy. I had no more strength left in me. Chintu took a step back. I dropped to my knees.

"Kenji, we have to fight! You have to move, damn it! Kenji, *Moooove!*" shouted inner me.

A burst of energy filled my body. I launched myself toward Chintu and brought him down with me.

"Why won't you just die?" Chintu shouted.

I held him down as tightly as my body would let me.

"Do it, Amariah!"

She ran to me as fast as her body would allow her to. She jumped, and with all her strength, she pushed the sword down through Chintu's heart and also mine. I placed the remains of my strength into my wings, grabbed Chintu, and flew up the hole to the world above. When I got to Valhalla, I dropped Chintu so everyone could see the monster he had become. With the sword still sticking through my chest, I knew that my time was coming to an end. I flew high, higher than ever before. Just so I could see the world one last time for what it was. I still didn't know what the purpose of life was or what I was meant to do with it. I felt sorrow. I never got to find out what I really was. Was I really a demon? Was I really a monster? I guessed it didn't matter anymore.

I closed my eyes, slowly sinking into that room where my inner self was. I walked through the darkness, and there he was. He looked more like a child than before.

"Kenji, you came back."

"I told myself I would make that dream of yours come true after all of this was over."

A door appeared from the darkness.

"Come. We don't have much time left."

I held his hand, and we walked through the door.

I opened my eyes and noticed how much more beautiful the world was now. So many more colors. I felt the heat of the sun hitting my body. For the first time in a long time, I felt something.

"Hey, Kenji, you see it too?"

"Yeah, it's beautiful!"

My power had run out. I started falling. The sword placed its curse on me. My body started to disintegrate into little bits of sand. I wondered what the world would think after I was gone.

* * *

Slowly, his body completely disintegrated, and Kenji was no longer.

The End

Milton Keynes UK
Ingram Content Group UK Ltd.
UKHW012148270923
429475UK00001B/52